D1505575

MAR   2015

MY LITTLE PONY

PONY TALES

featuring PINKIE PIE

STORY BY **Ted Anderson**

ART and COLORS BY **Ben Bates**

LETTERS BY **Neil Uyetake**

 Spotlight

ABDOPUBLISHING.COM

Reinforced library bound edition published in 2015 by Spotlight,
a division of ABDO, PO Box 398166, Minneapolis, Minnesota 55439.
Spotlight produces high-quality reinforced library bound editions for
schools and libraries. Published by agreement with IDW.

Printed in the United States of America, North Mankato, Minnesota.
112014
012015

THIS BOOK CONTAINS
RECYCLED MATERIALS

LIBRARY OF CONGRESS CATALOGING-IN-PUBLICATION DATA

Anderson, Ted, 1985-
  Pinkie Pie / writer, Ted Anderson ; artist, Ben Bates. -- Reinforced library
bound edition.
      pages cm. -- (My little pony. Pony tales)
  Summary: "Pinkie Pie wins tickets to a famous clown's show"-- Provided by
publisher.
  ISBN 978-1-61479-333-5
1. Graphic novels. I. Bates, Ben, 1982- illustrator. II. Title.
  PZ7.7.A49Pi 2015
  741.5'973--dc23

                    2014036760

Spotlight

A Division of ABDO
abdopublishing.com

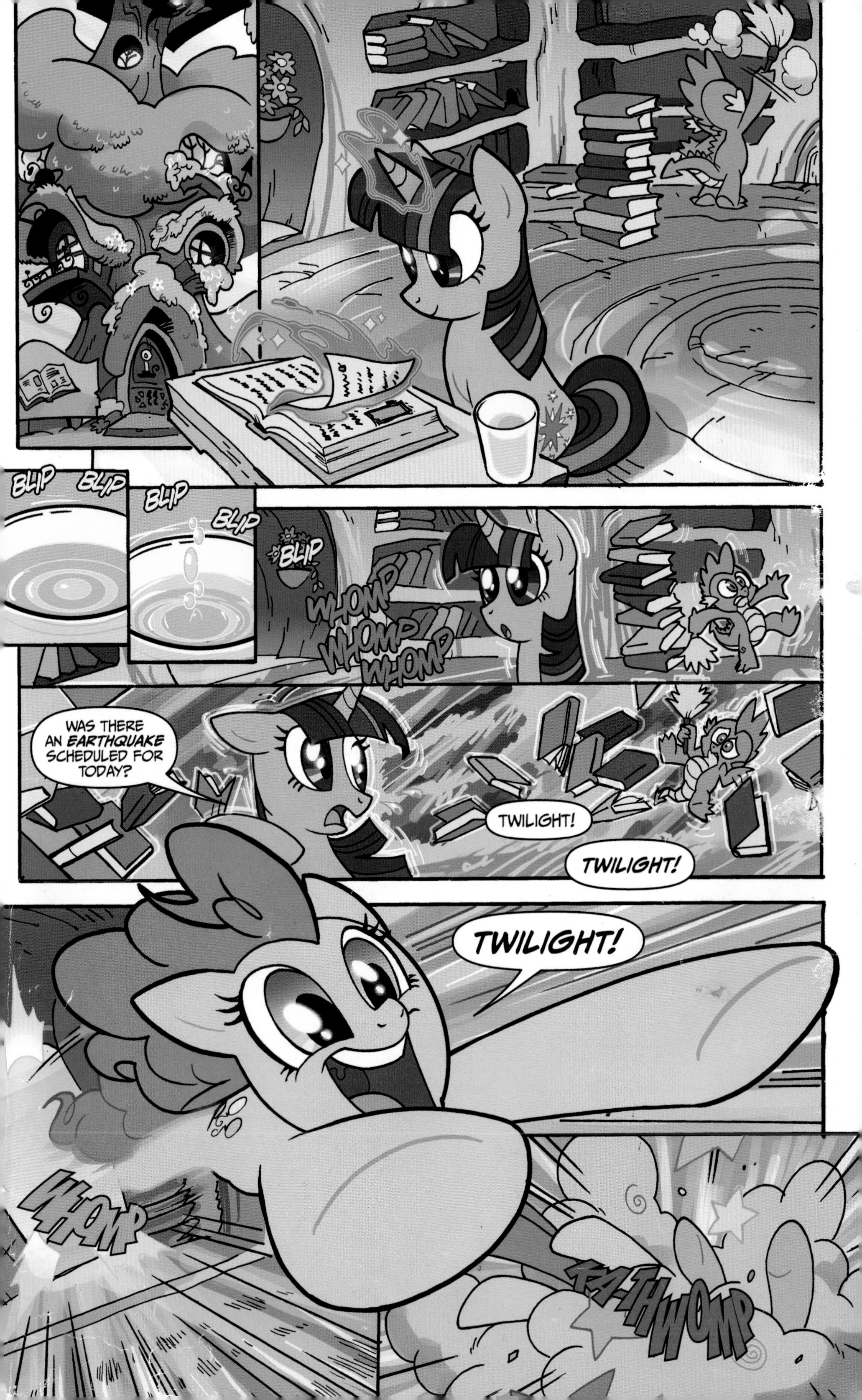

BLIP
BLIP
BLIP
BLIP
BLIP
WHOMP
WHOMP
WHOMP
WAS THERE AN EARTHQUAKE SCHEDULED FOR TODAY?
TWILIGHT!
TWILIGHT!
TWILIGHT!
WHOMP
KA-THWOMP

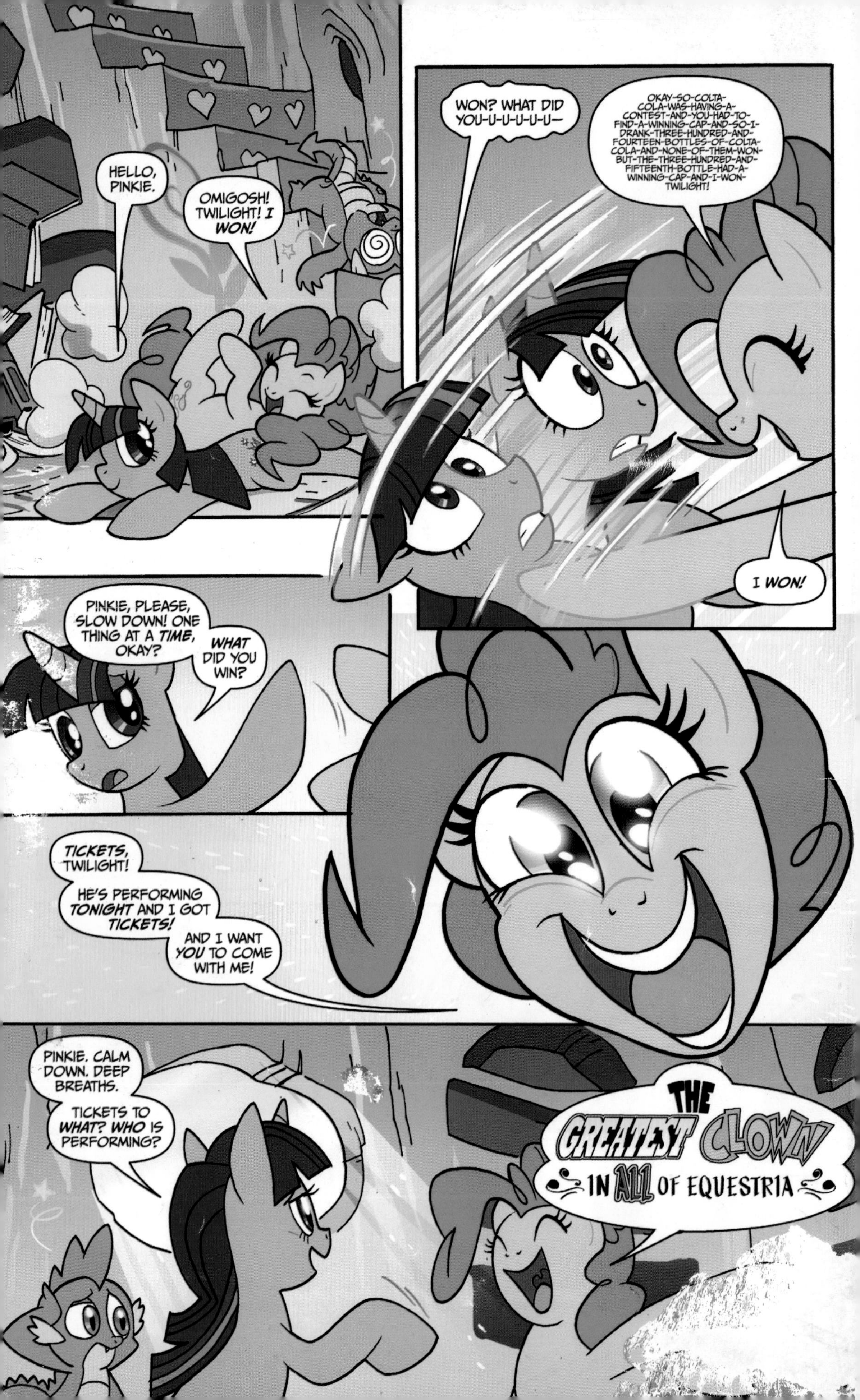

HELLO, PINKIE.
OMIGOSH! TWILIGHT! I WON!
WON? WHAT DID YOU-U-U-U-U-U—
OKAY-SO-COLTA-COLA-WAS-HAVING-A-CONTEST-AND-YOU-HAD-TO-FIND-A-WINNING-CAP-AND-SO-I-DRANK-THREE-HUNDRED-AND-FOURTEEN-BOTTLES-OF-COLTA-COLA-AND-NONE-OF-THEM-WON-BUT-THE-THREE-HUNDRED-AND-FIFTEENTH-BOTTLE-HAD-A-WINNING-CAP-AND-I-WON-TWILIGHT!
I WON!
PINKIE, PLEASE, SLOW DOWN! ONE THING AT A TIME, OKAY?
WHAT DID YOU WIN?
TICKETS, TWILIGHT!
HE'S PERFORMING TONIGHT AND I GOT TICKETS!
AND I WANT YOU TO COME WITH ME!
PINKIE. CALM DOWN. DEEP BREATHS.
TICKETS TO WHAT? WHO IS PERFORMING?
THE GREATEST CLOWN IN ALL OF EQUESTRIA

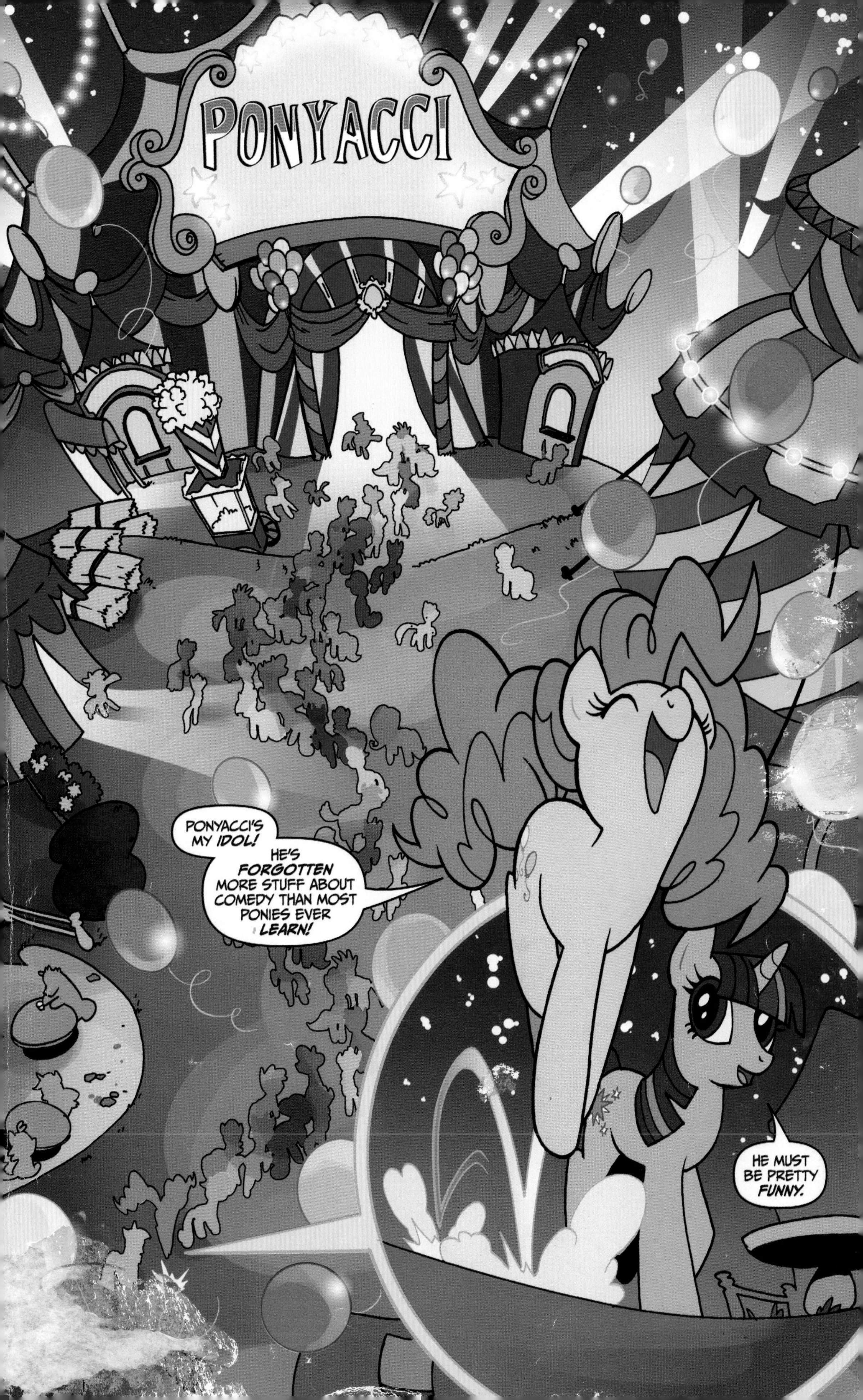
PONYACCI
PONYACCI'S MY *IDOL!*
HE'S *FORGOTTEN* MORE STUFF ABOUT COMEDY THAN MOST PONIES EVER *LEARN!*
HE MUST BE PRETTY *FUNNY.*

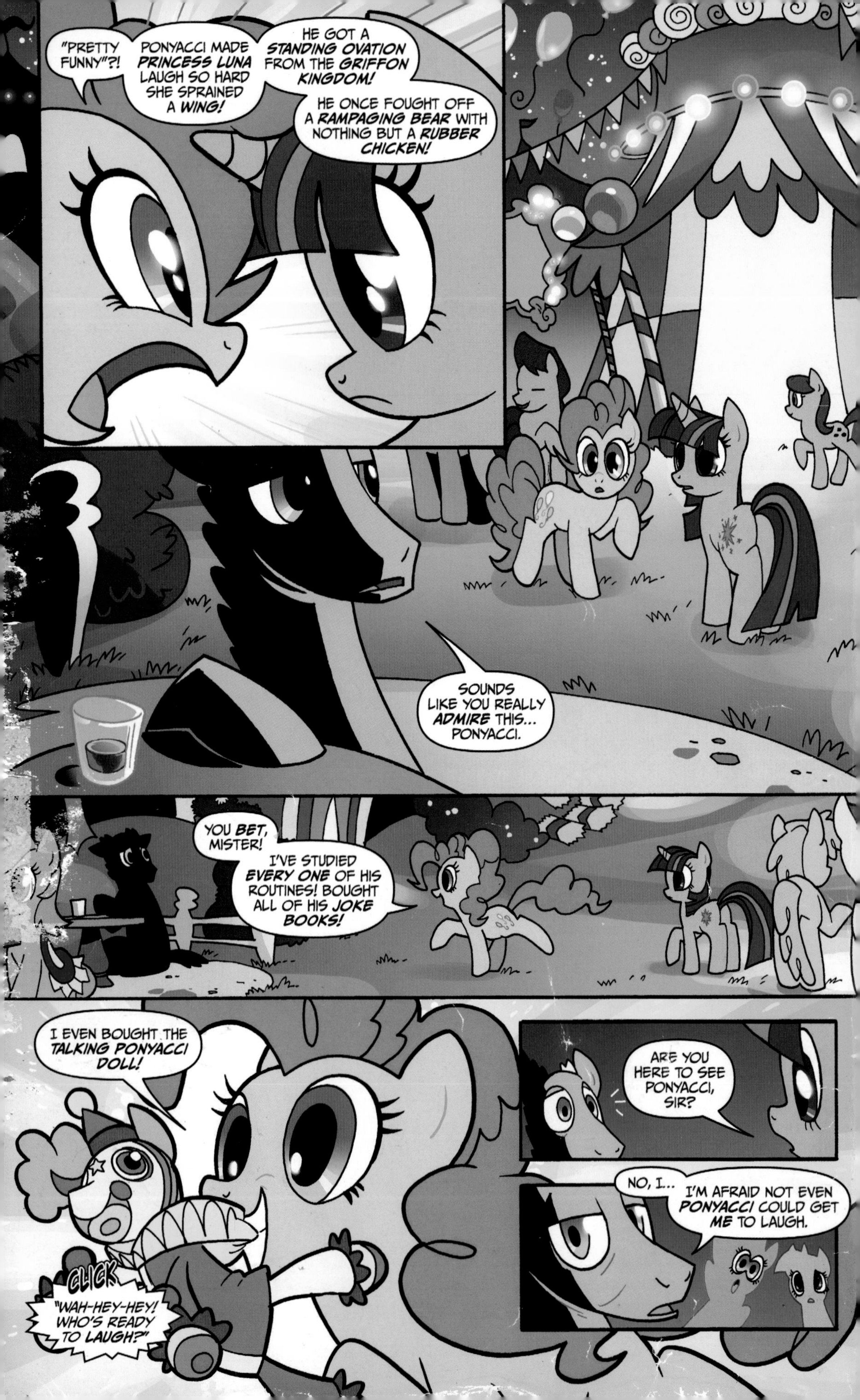

"PRETTY FUNNY"?!
PONYACCI MADE PRINCESS LUNA LAUGH SO HARD SHE SPRAINED A WING!
HE GOT A STANDING OVATION FROM THE GRIFFON KINGDOM!
HE ONCE FOUGHT OFF A RAMPAGING BEAR WITH NOTHING BUT A RUBBER CHICKEN!
SOUNDS LIKE YOU REALLY ADMIRE THIS... PONYACCI.
YOU BET, MISTER!
I'VE STUDIED EVERY ONE OF HIS ROUTINES! BOUGHT ALL OF HIS JOKE BOOKS!
I EVEN BOUGHT THE TALKING PONYACCI DOLL!
CLICK
"WAH-HEY-HEY! WHO'S READY TO LAUGH?"
ARE YOU HERE TO SEE PONYACCI, SIR?
NO, I...
I'M AFRAID NOT EVEN PONYACCI COULD GET ME TO LAUGH.

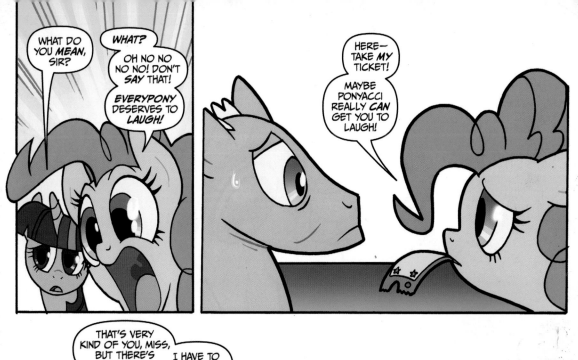

WHAT DO YOU *MEAN*, SIR?

WHAT? OH NO NO NO NO! DON'T *SAY* THAT! *EVERYPONY* DESERVES TO LAUGH!

HERE—TAKE *MY* TICKET! MAYBE PONYACCI REALLY *CAN* GET YOU TO LAUGH!

THAT'S VERY KIND OF YOU, MISS, BUT THERE'S NO NEED. I HAVE TO GO—ENJOY THE SHOW.

COME ON, PINKIE. THE SHOW'S ABOUT TO START.

FILLIES AND GENTLECOLTS! FOALS OF ALL AGES!

PREPARE YOURSELF FOR THE *ASTOUNDING ANTICS* OF EQUESTRIA'S SILLIEST STAR...

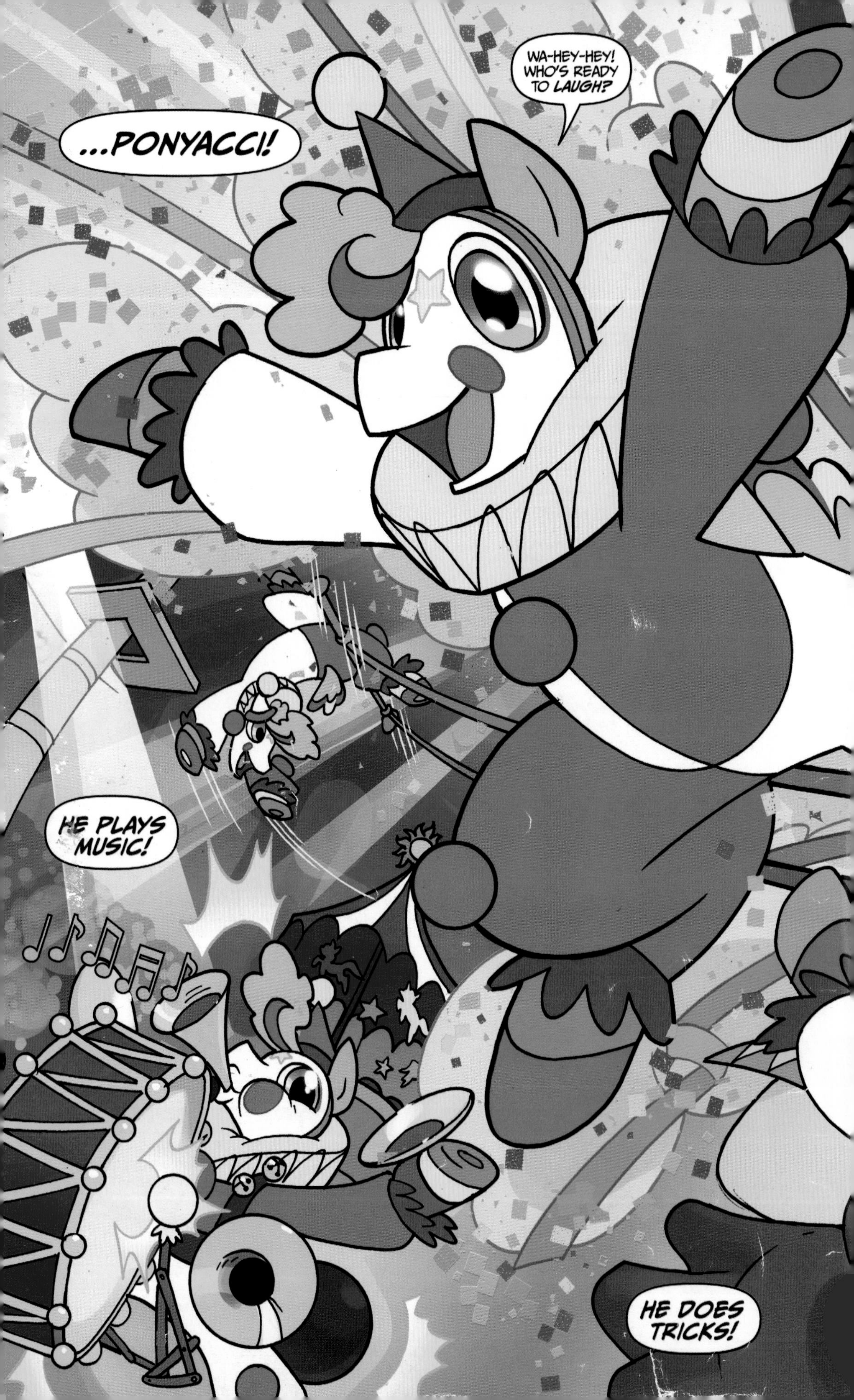
...PONYACCI!
WA-HEY-HEY! WHO'S READY TO LAUGH?
HE PLAYS MUSIC!
HE DOES TRICKS!

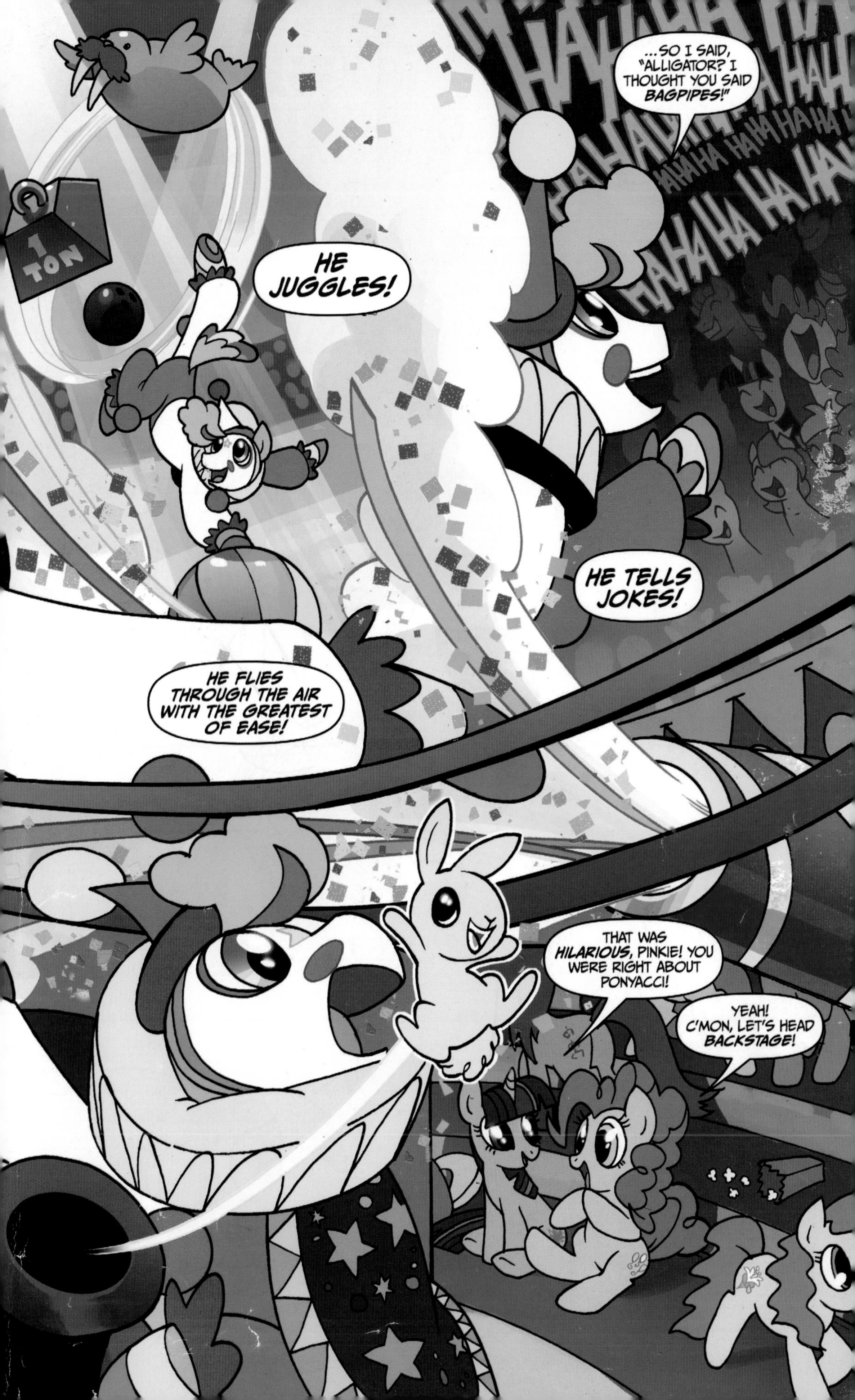
...SO I SAID, "ALLIGATOR? I THOUGHT YOU SAID BAGPIPES!"
HAHAHAHAHA HAHAHA HA HA HAHAHA HA HA HA HA HA
HE JUGGLES!
HE TELLS JOKES!
HE FLIES THROUGH THE AIR WITH THE GREATEST OF EASE!
1 TON
THAT WAS HILARIOUS, PINKIE! YOU WERE RIGHT ABOUT PONYACCI!
YEAH! C'MON, LET'S HEAD BACKSTAGE!

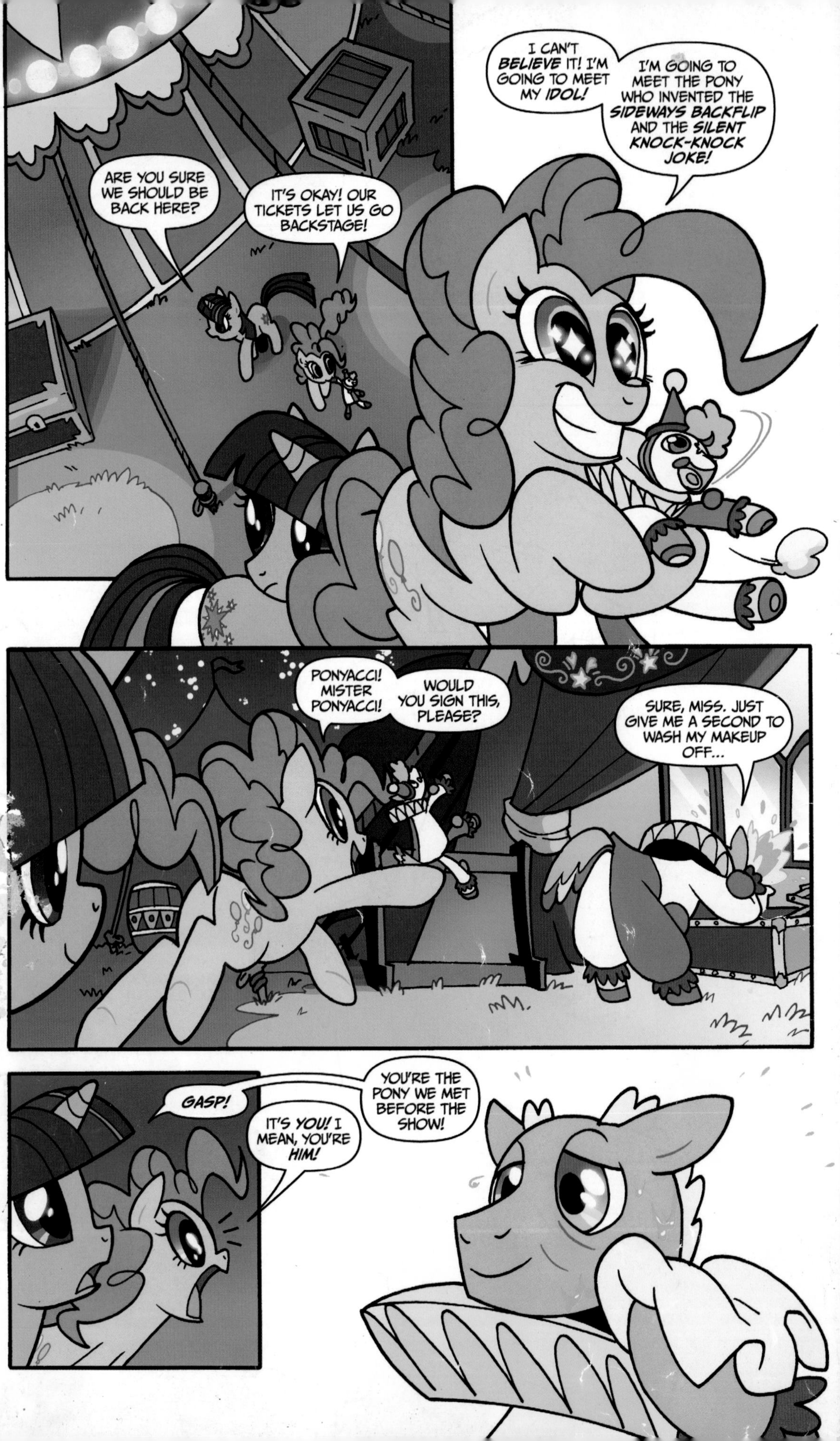
I CAN'T BELIEVE IT! I'M GOING TO MEET MY IDOL!
I'M GOING TO MEET THE PONY WHO INVENTED THE SIDEWAYS BACKFLIP AND THE SILENT KNOCK-KNOCK JOKE!
ARE YOU SURE WE SHOULD BE BACK HERE?
IT'S OKAY! OUR TICKETS LET US GO BACKSTAGE!
PONYACCI! MISTER PONYACCI!
WOULD YOU SIGN THIS, PLEASE?
SURE, MISS. JUST GIVE ME A SECOND TO WASH MY MAKEUP OFF...
GASP!
IT'S YOU! I MEAN, YOU'RE HIM!
YOU'RE THE PONY WE MET BEFORE THE SHOW!

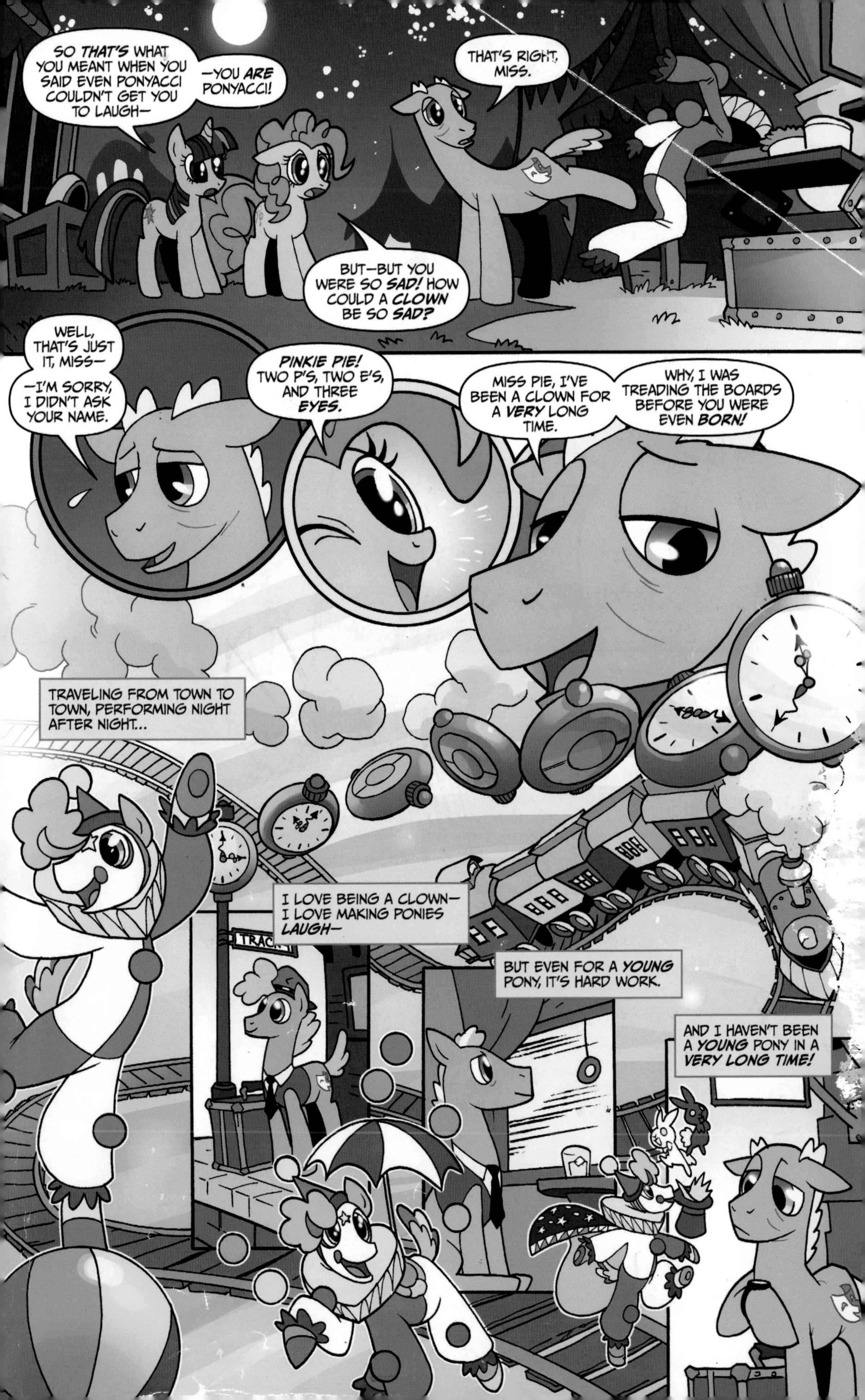
SO THAT'S WHAT YOU MEANT WHEN YOU SAID EVEN PONYACCI COULDN'T GET YOU TO LAUGH—
—YOU ARE PONYACCI!
THAT'S RIGHT, MISS.
BUT—BUT YOU WERE SO SAD! HOW COULD A CLOWN BE SO SAD?
WELL, THAT'S JUST IT, MISS—
—I'M SORRY, I DIDN'T ASK YOUR NAME.
PINKIE PIE! TWO P'S, TWO E'S, AND THREE EYES.
MISS PIE, I'VE BEEN A CLOWN FOR A VERY LONG TIME.
WHY, I WAS TREADING THE BOARDS BEFORE YOU WERE EVEN BORN!
TRAVELING FROM TOWN TO TOWN, PERFORMING NIGHT AFTER NIGHT...
I LOVE BEING A CLOWN— I LOVE MAKING PONIES LAUGH—
BUT EVEN FOR A YOUNG PONY, IT'S HARD WORK.
AND I HAVEN'T BEEN A YOUNG PONY IN A VERY LONG TIME!

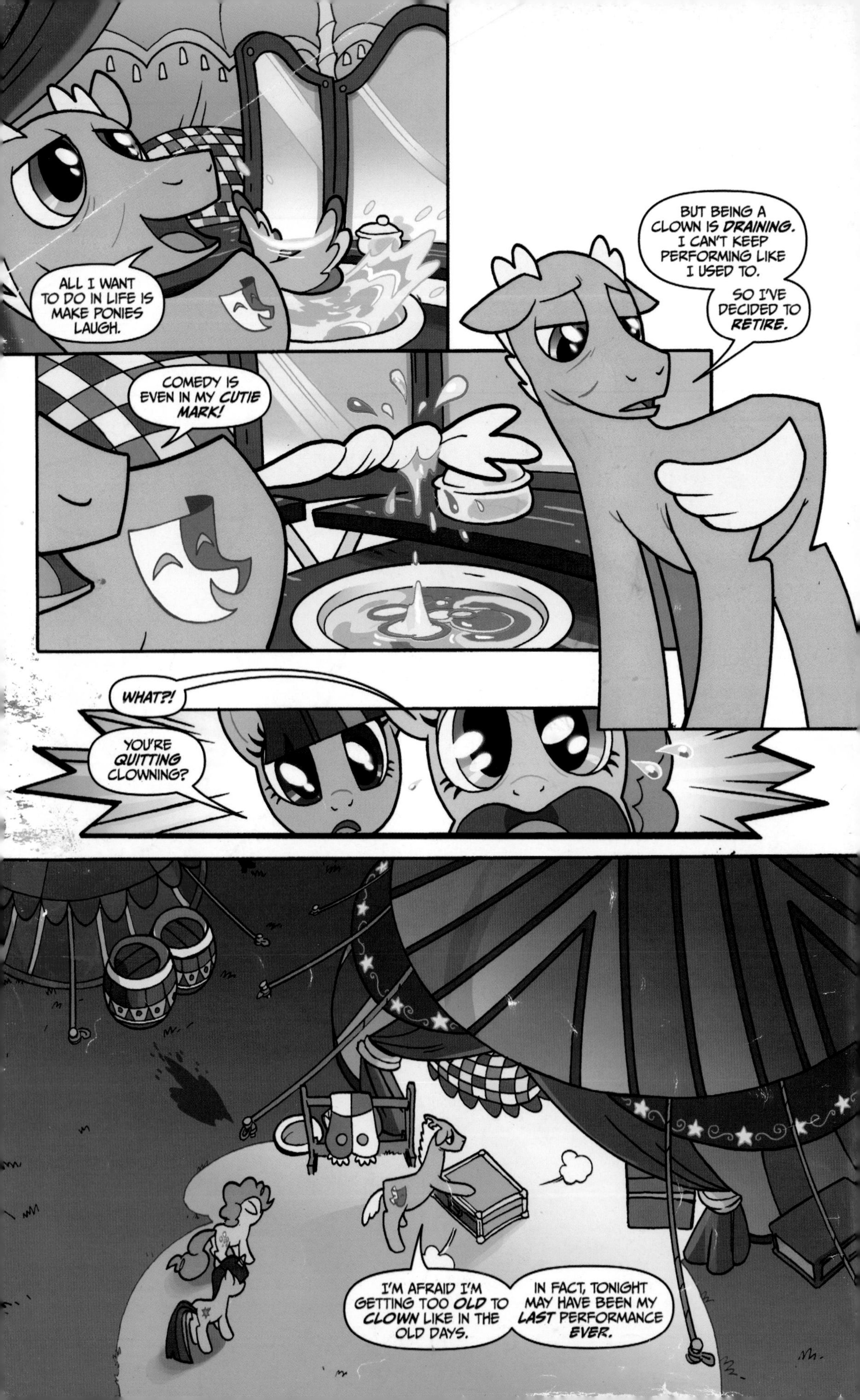
ALL I WANT TO DO IN LIFE IS MAKE PONIES LAUGH.
COMEDY IS EVEN IN MY CUTIE MARK!
BUT BEING A CLOWN IS DRAINING. I CAN'T KEEP PERFORMING LIKE I USED TO.
SO I'VE DECIDED TO RETIRE.
WHAT?!
YOU'RE QUITTING CLOWNING?
I'M AFRAID I'M GETTING TOO OLD TO CLOWN LIKE IN THE OLD DAYS.
IN FACT, TONIGHT MAY HAVE BEEN MY LAST PERFORMANCE EVER.

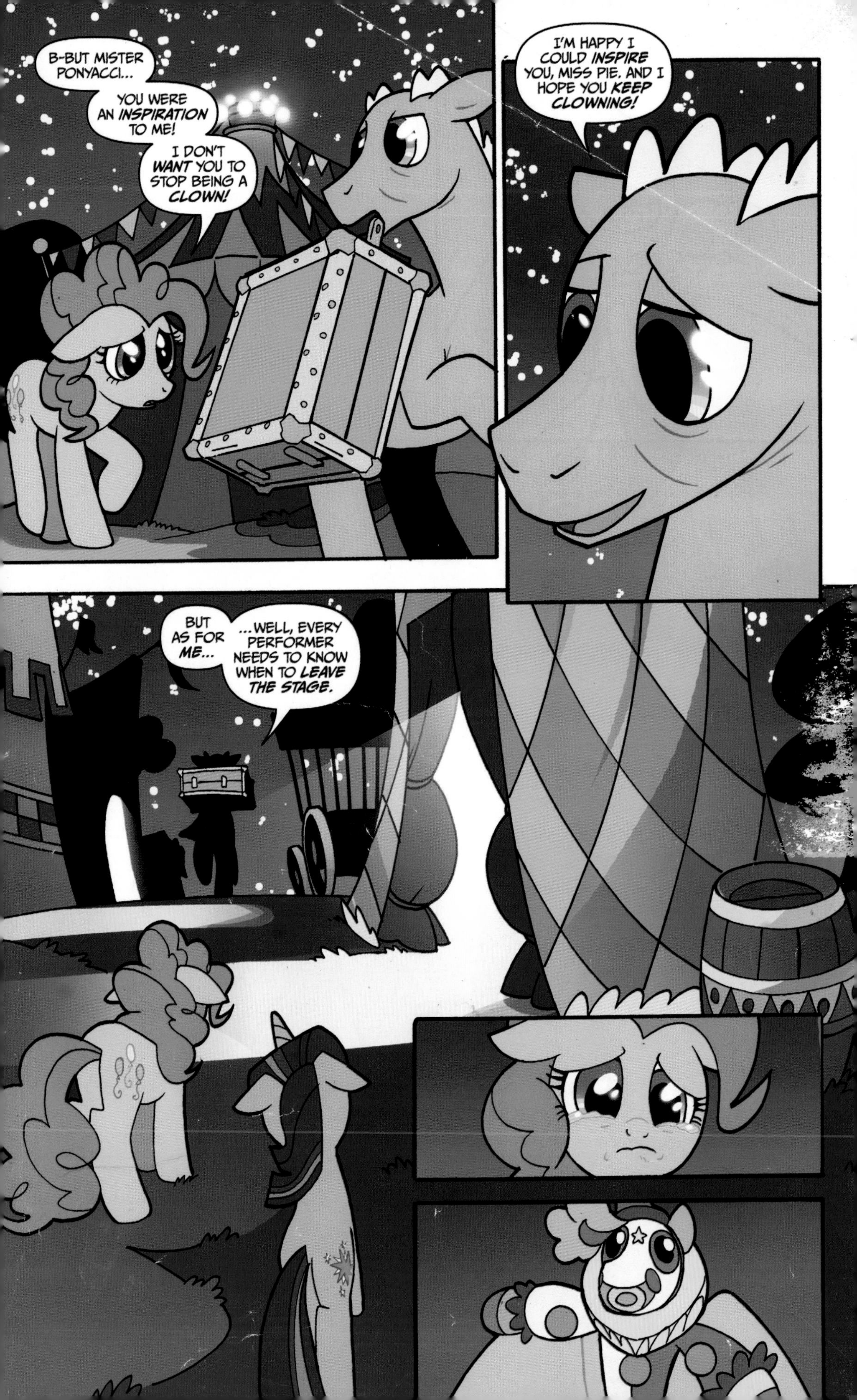
B-BUT MISTER PONYACCI...
YOU WERE AN *INSPIRATION* TO ME!
I DON'T *WANT* YOU TO STOP BEING A *CLOWN!*
I'M HAPPY I COULD *INSPIRE* YOU, MISS PIE. AND I HOPE YOU *KEEP CLOWNING!*
BUT AS FOR *ME...*
...WELL, EVERY PERFORMER NEEDS TO KNOW WHEN TO *LEAVE THE STAGE.*

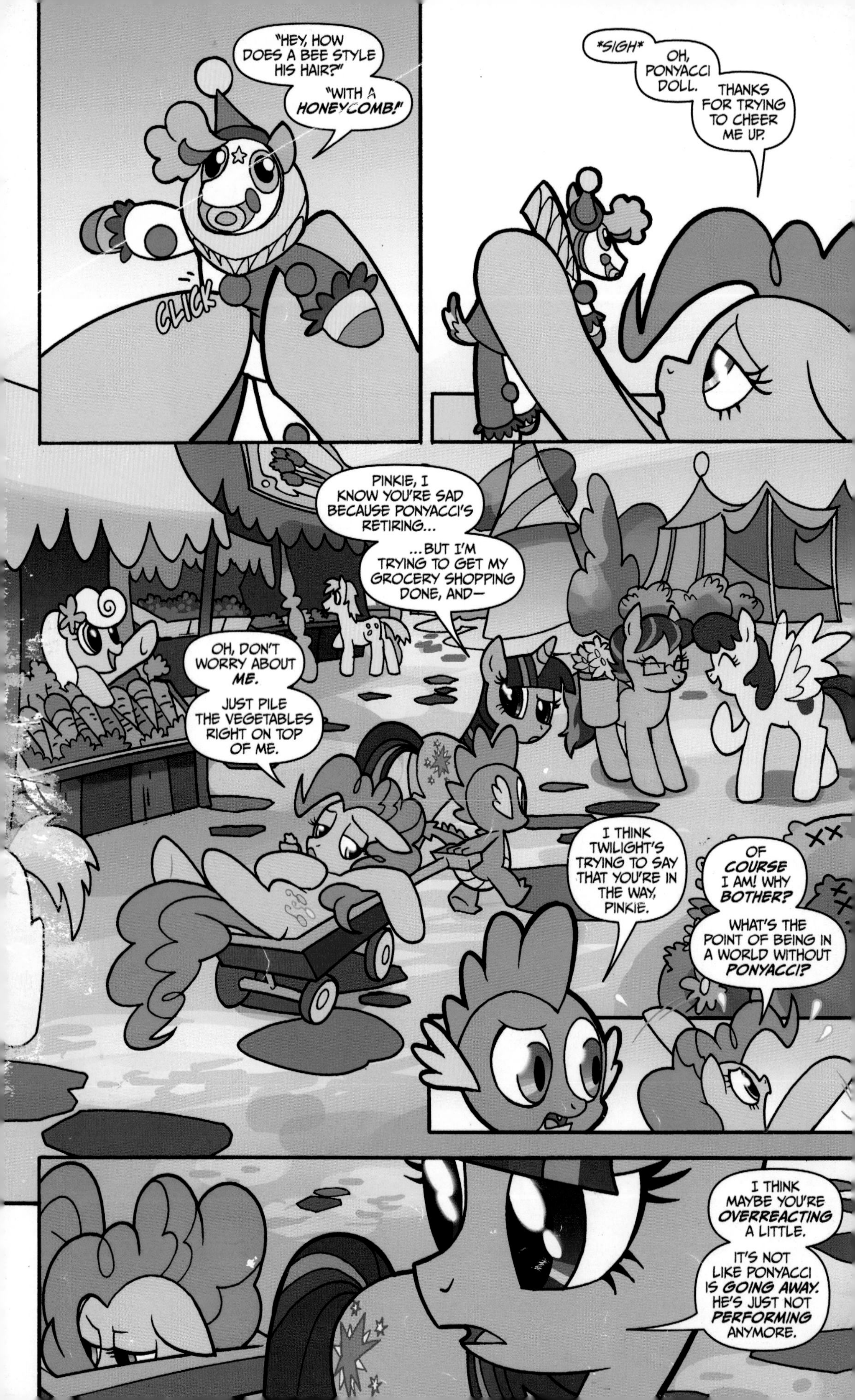
"HEY, HOW DOES A BEE STYLE HIS HAIR?"
"WITH A HONEYCOMB!"
CLICK
SIGH
OH, PONYACCI DOLL.
THANKS FOR TRYING TO CHEER ME UP.
PINKIE, I KNOW YOU'RE SAD BECAUSE PONYACCI'S RETIRING...
...BUT I'M TRYING TO GET MY GROCERY SHOPPING DONE, AND—
OH, DON'T WORRY ABOUT ME.
JUST PILE THE VEGETABLES RIGHT ON TOP OF ME.
I THINK TWILIGHT'S TRYING TO SAY THAT YOU'RE IN THE WAY, PINKIE.
OF COURSE I AM! WHY BOTHER?
WHAT'S THE POINT OF BEING IN A WORLD WITHOUT PONYACCI?
I THINK MAYBE YOU'RE OVERREACTING A LITTLE.
IT'S NOT LIKE PONYACCI IS GOING AWAY. HE'S JUST NOT PERFORMING ANYMORE.

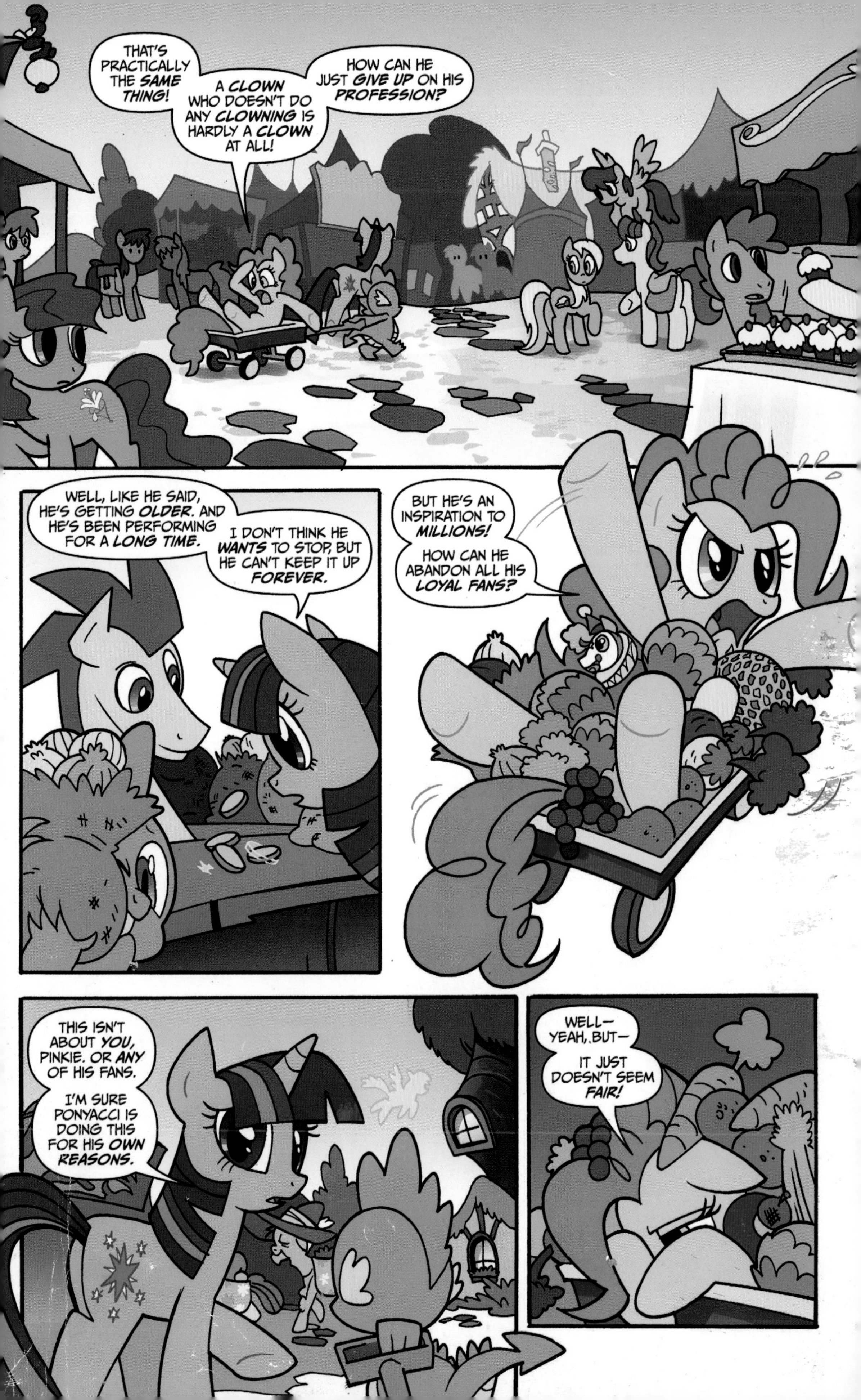

THAT'S PRACTICALLY THE SAME THING!
A CLOWN WHO DOESN'T DO ANY CLOWNING IS HARDLY A CLOWN AT ALL!
HOW CAN HE JUST GIVE UP ON HIS PROFESSION?
WELL, LIKE HE SAID, HE'S GETTING OLDER. AND HE'S BEEN PERFORMING FOR A LONG TIME.
I DON'T THINK HE WANTS TO STOP, BUT HE CAN'T KEEP IT UP FOREVER.
BUT HE'S AN INSPIRATION TO MILLIONS!
HOW CAN HE ABANDON ALL HIS LOYAL FANS?
THIS ISN'T ABOUT YOU, PINKIE. OR ANY OF HIS FANS.
I'M SURE PONYACCI IS DOING THIS FOR HIS OWN REASONS.
WELL— YEAH, BUT—
IT JUST DOESN'T SEEM FAIR!

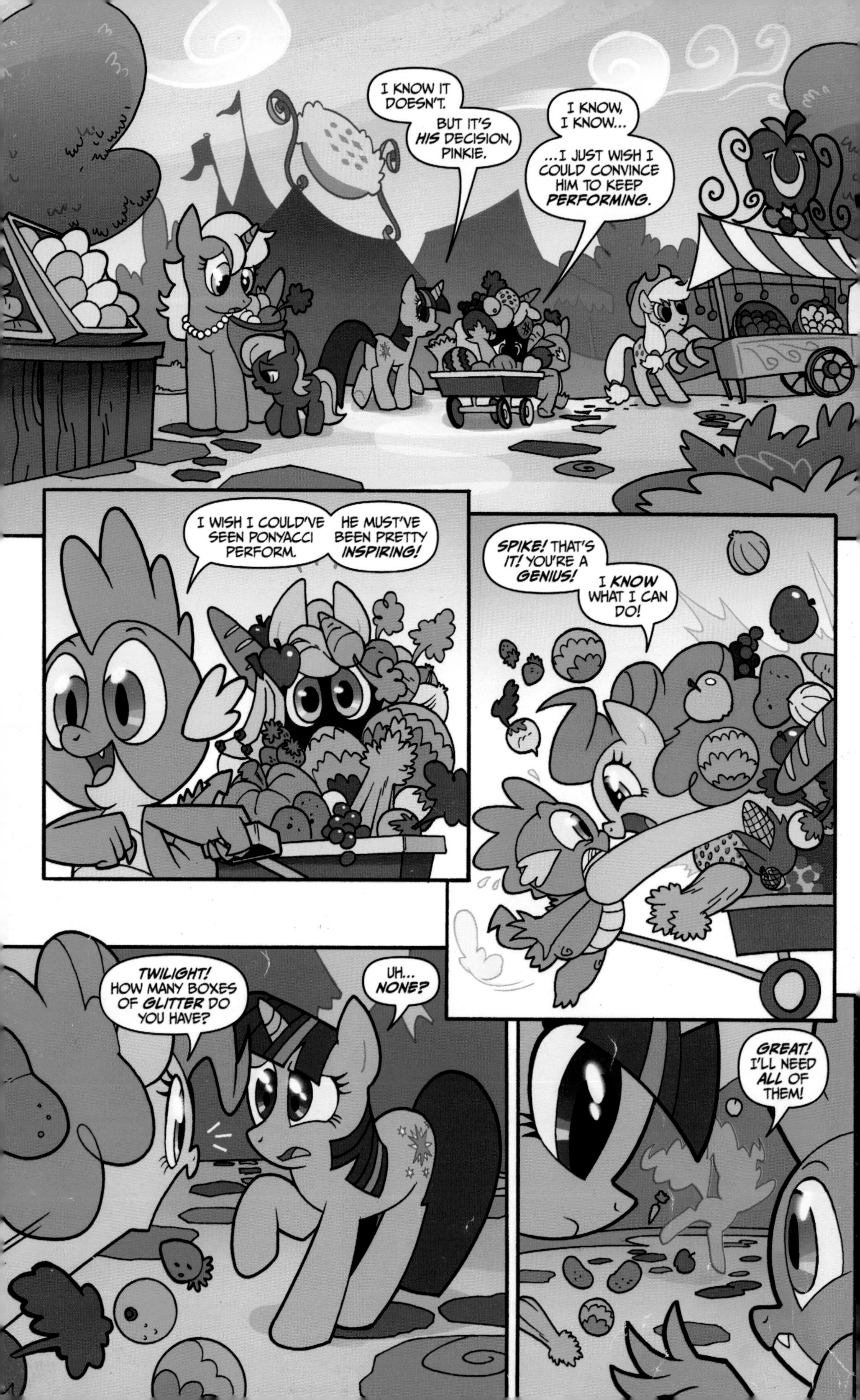
I KNOW IT DOESN'T.
BUT IT'S *HIS* DECISION, PINKIE.
I KNOW, I KNOW...
...I JUST WISH I COULD CONVINCE HIM TO KEEP *PERFORMING*.
I WISH I COULD'VE SEEN PONYACCI PERFORM.
HE MUST'VE BEEN PRETTY *INSPIRING!*
SPIKE! THAT'S *IT!* YOU'RE A *GENIUS!*
I *KNOW* WHAT I CAN DO!
TWILIGHT! HOW MANY BOXES OF *GLITTER* DO YOU HAVE?
UH... *NONE?*
GREAT! I'LL NEED *ALL* OF THEM!

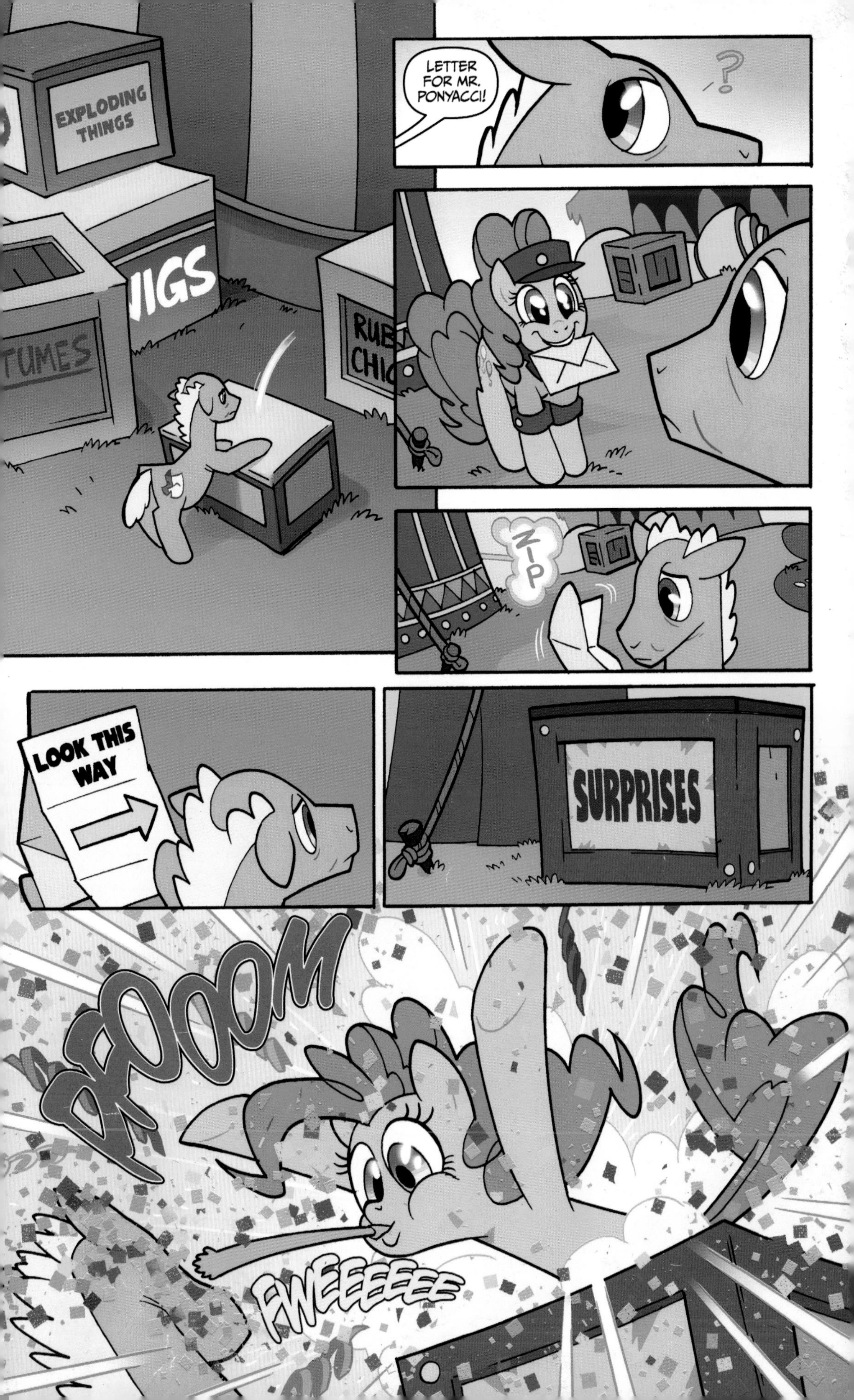
EXPLODING THINGS
WIGS
TUMES
RUB CHIC
LETTER FOR MR. PONYACCI!
?
ZIP
LOOK THIS WAY
SURPRISES
BOOOOM
FWEEEEEE

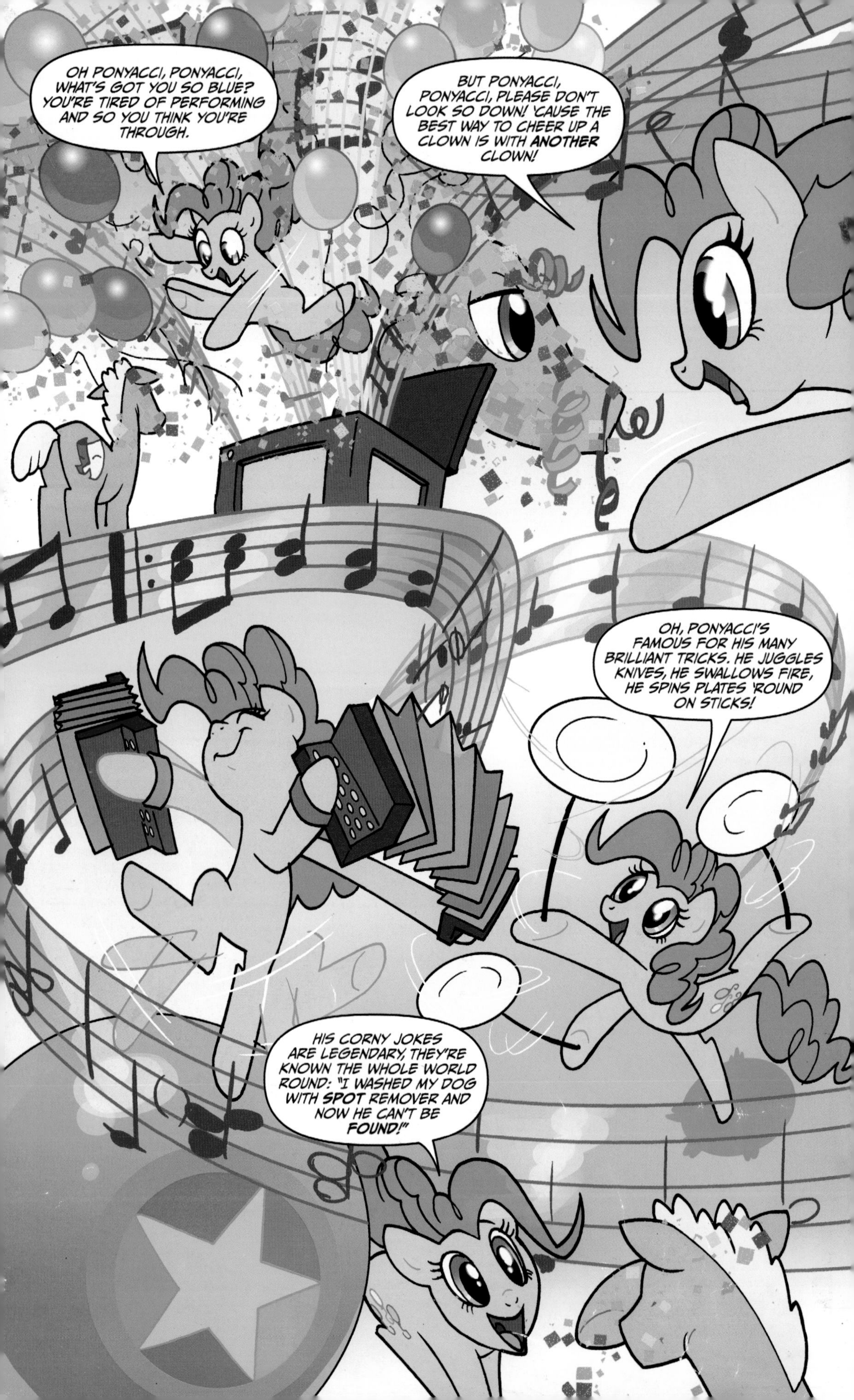
OH PONYACCI, PONYACCI, WHAT'S GOT YOU SO BLUE? YOU'RE TIRED OF PERFORMING AND SO YOU THINK YOU'RE THROUGH.
BUT PONYACCI, PONYACCI, PLEASE DON'T LOOK SO DOWN! 'CAUSE THE BEST WAY TO CHEER UP A CLOWN IS WITH ANOTHER CLOWN!
OH, PONYACCI'S FAMOUS FOR HIS MANY BRILLIANT TRICKS. HE JUGGLES KNIVES, HE SWALLOWS FIRE, HE SPINS PLATES 'ROUND ON STICKS!
HIS CORNY JOKES ARE LEGENDARY, THEY'RE KNOWN THE WHOLE WORLD ROUND: "I WASHED MY DOG WITH SPOT REMOVER AND NOW HE CAN'T BE FOUND!"

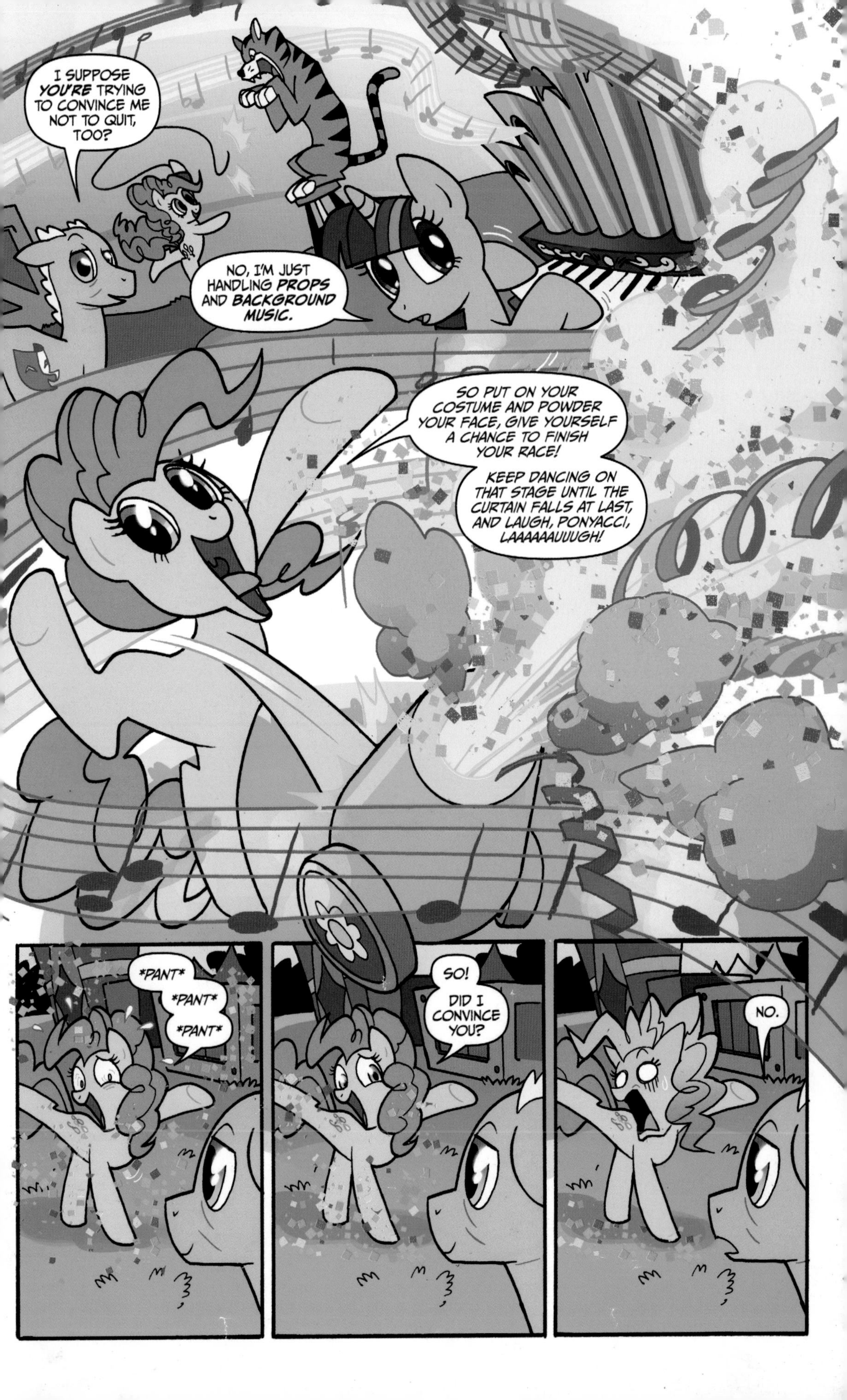
I SUPPOSE YOU'RE TRYING TO CONVINCE ME NOT TO QUIT, TOO?
NO, I'M JUST HANDLING PROPS AND BACKGROUND MUSIC.
SO PUT ON YOUR COSTUME AND POWDER YOUR FACE, GIVE YOURSELF A CHANCE TO FINISH YOUR RACE!
KEEP DANCING ON THAT STAGE UNTIL THE CURTAIN FALLS AT LAST, AND LAUGH, PONYACCI, LAAAAAAUUUGH!
PANT *PANT* *PANT*
SO! DID I CONVINCE YOU?
NO.

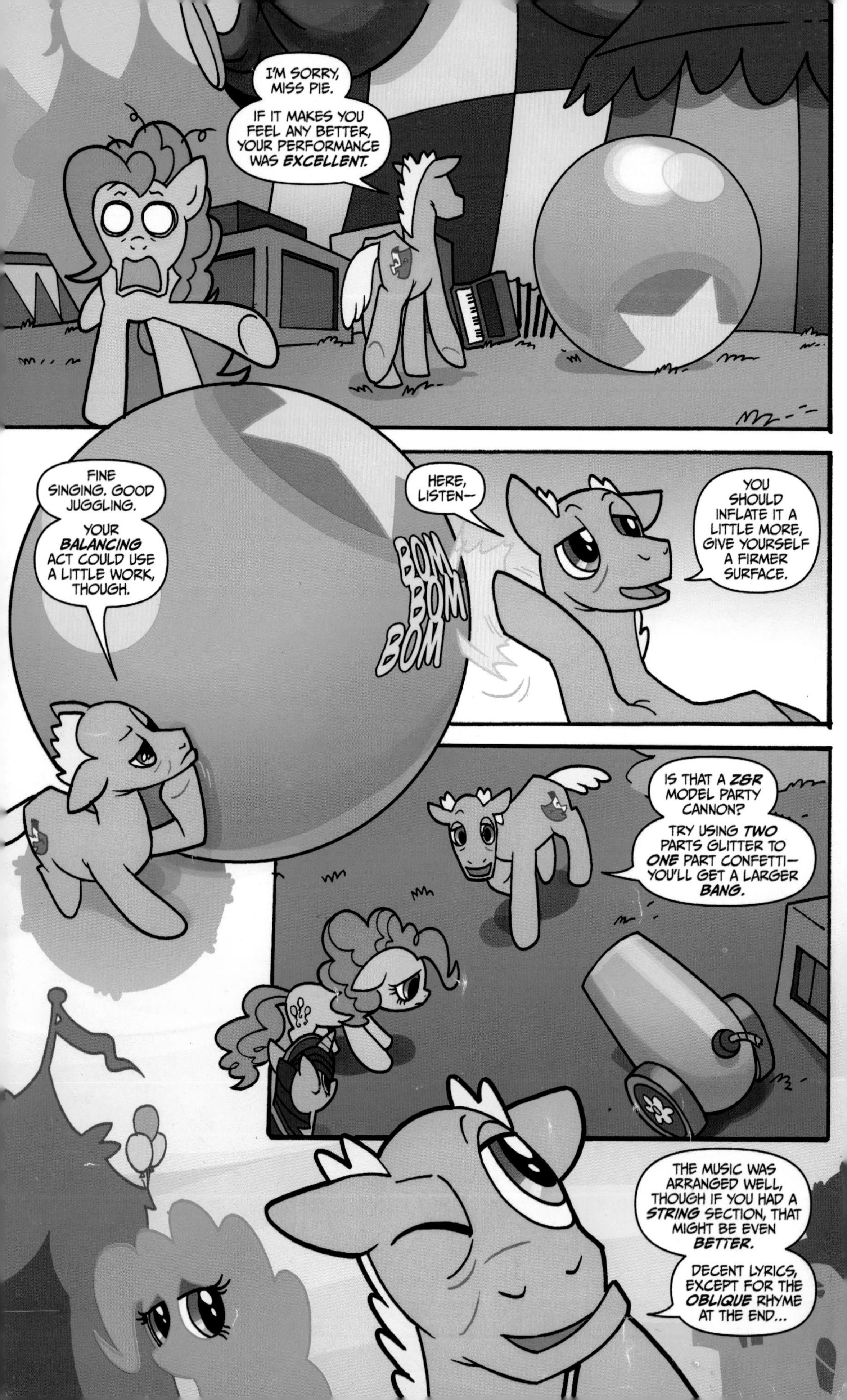
I'M SORRY, MISS PIE.
IF IT MAKES YOU FEEL ANY BETTER, YOUR PERFORMANCE WAS EXCELLENT.
FINE SINGING. GOOD JUGGLING.
YOUR BALANCING ACT COULD USE A LITTLE WORK, THOUGH.
HERE, LISTEN—
BOM BOM BOM
YOU SHOULD INFLATE IT A LITTLE MORE, GIVE YOURSELF A FIRMER SURFACE.
IS THAT A Z&R MODEL PARTY CANNON?
TRY USING TWO PARTS GLITTER TO ONE PART CONFETTI— YOU'LL GET A LARGER BANG.
THE MUSIC WAS ARRANGED WELL, THOUGH IF YOU HAD A STRING SECTION, THAT MIGHT BE EVEN BETTER.
DECENT LYRICS, EXCEPT FOR THE OBLIQUE RHYME AT THE END...

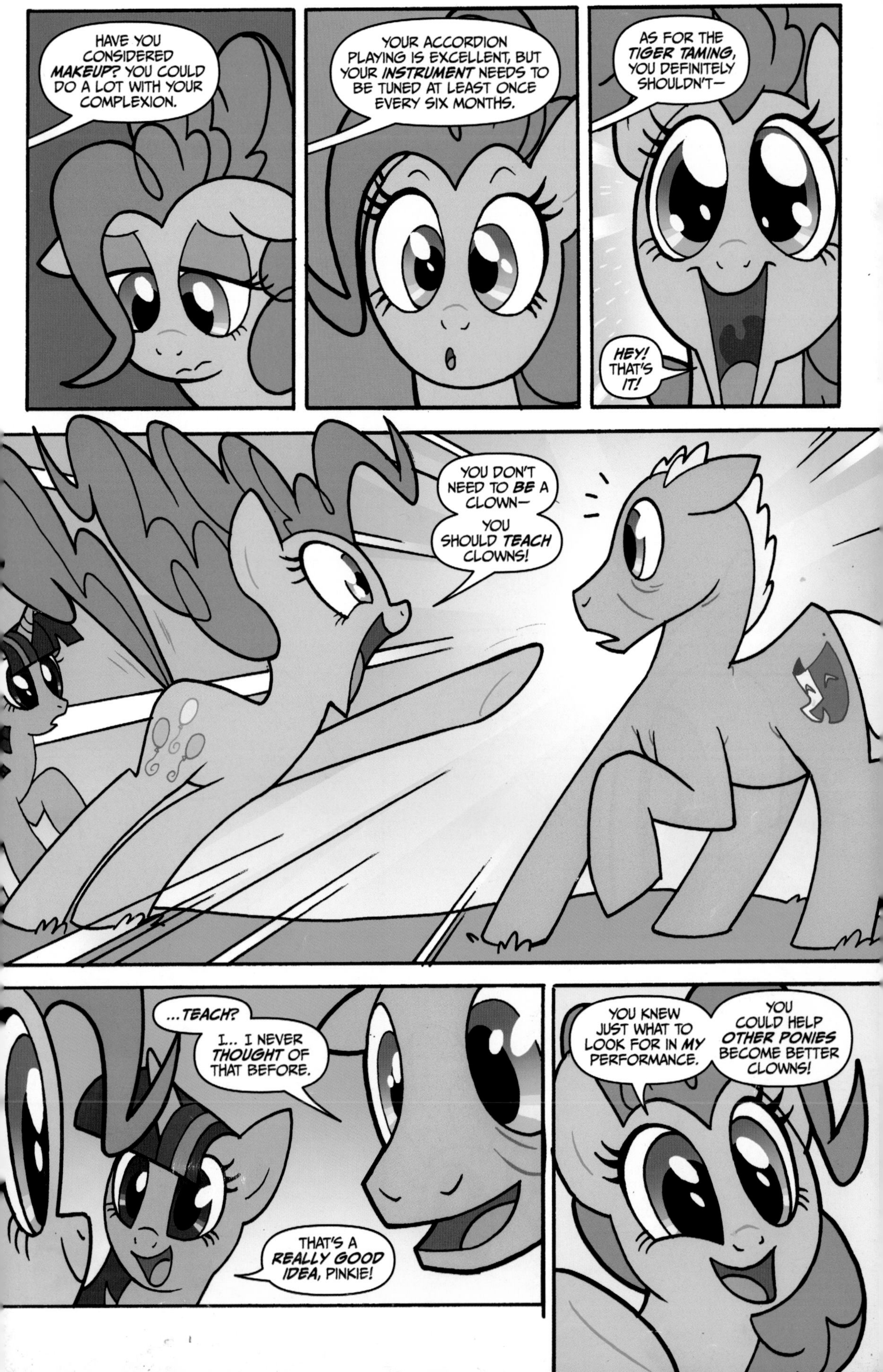
HAVE YOU CONSIDERED MAKEUP? YOU COULD DO A LOT WITH YOUR COMPLEXION.
YOUR ACCORDION PLAYING IS EXCELLENT, BUT YOUR INSTRUMENT NEEDS TO BE TUNED AT LEAST ONCE EVERY SIX MONTHS.
AS FOR THE TIGER TAMING, YOU DEFINITELY SHOULDN'T—
HEY! THAT'S IT!
YOU DON'T NEED TO BE A CLOWN—
YOU SHOULD TEACH CLOWNS!
...TEACH?
I... I NEVER THOUGHT OF THAT BEFORE.
THAT'S A REALLY GOOD IDEA, PINKIE!
YOU KNEW JUST WHAT TO LOOK FOR IN MY PERFORMANCE.
YOU COULD HELP OTHER PONIES BECOME BETTER CLOWNS!

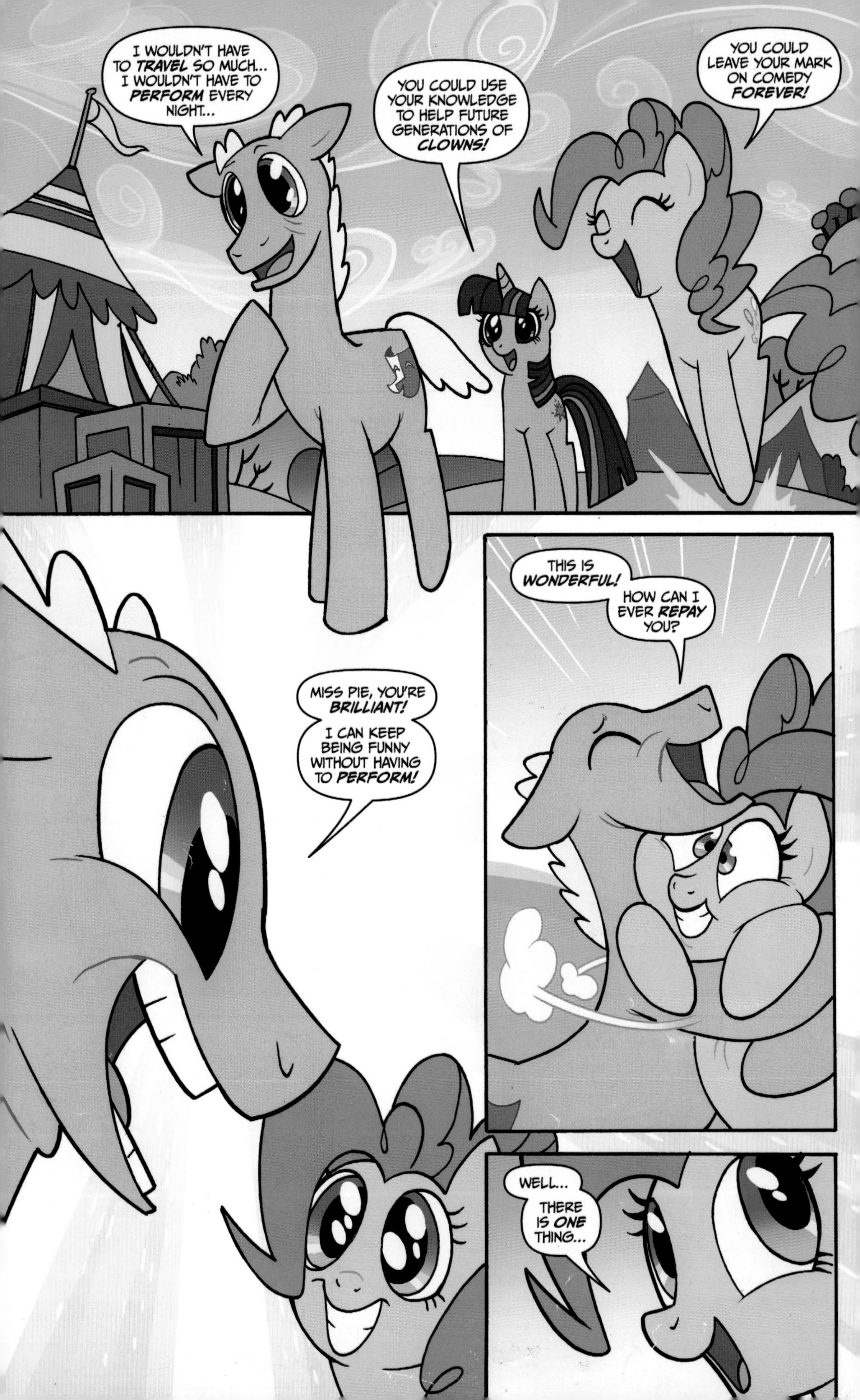

I WOULDN'T HAVE TO TRAVEL SO MUCH... I WOULDN'T HAVE TO PERFORM EVERY NIGHT...
YOU COULD USE YOUR KNOWLEDGE TO HELP FUTURE GENERATIONS OF CLOWNS!
YOU COULD LEAVE YOUR MARK ON COMEDY FOREVER!
MISS PIE, YOU'RE BRILLIANT!
I CAN KEEP BEING FUNNY WITHOUT HAVING TO PERFORM!
THIS IS WONDERFUL!
HOW CAN I EVER REPAY YOU?
WELL...
THERE IS ONE THING...

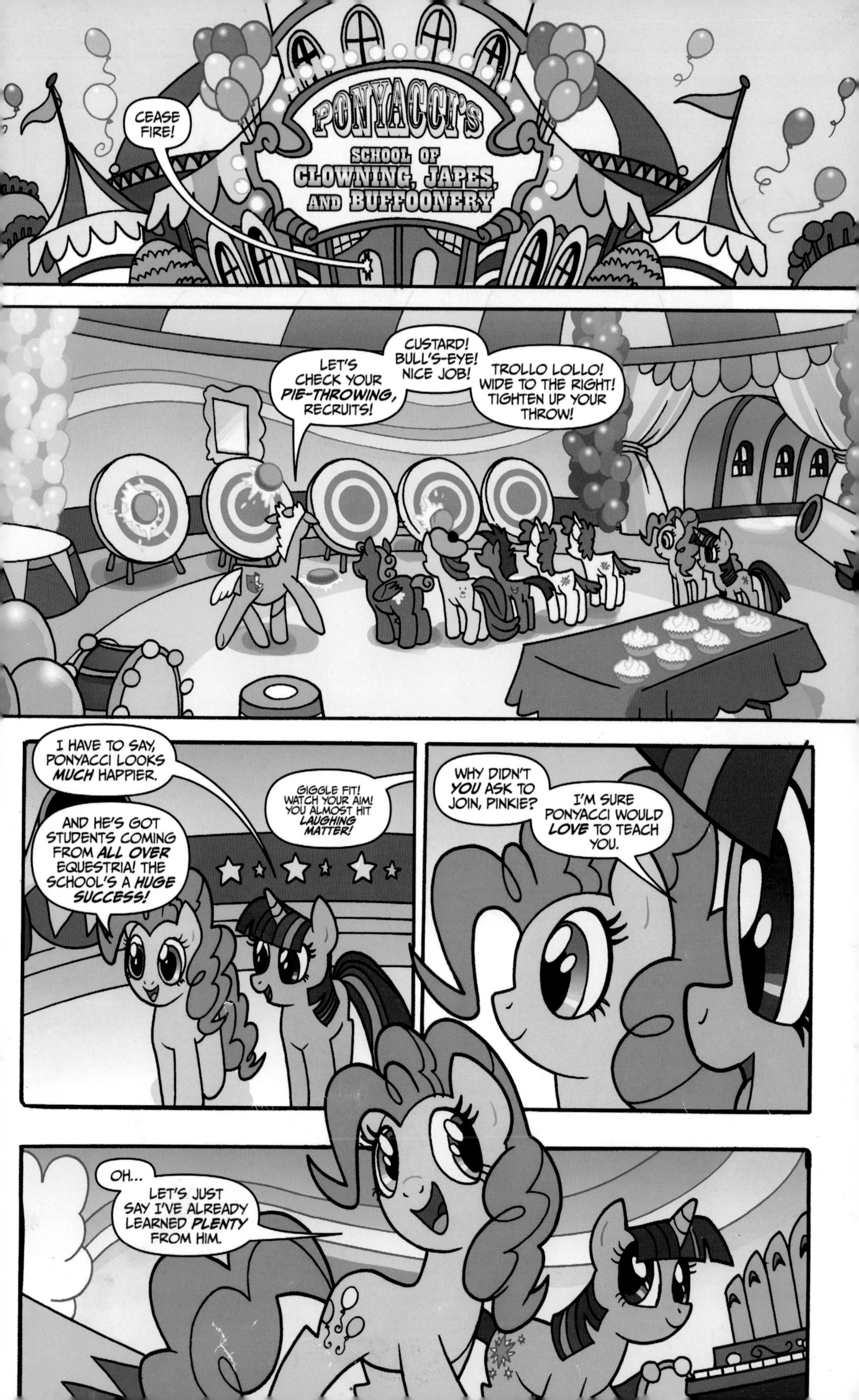
PONYACCI'S
SCHOOL OF
CLOWNING, JAPES, AND BUFFOONERY
CEASE FIRE!
LET'S CHECK YOUR PIE-THROWING, RECRUITS!
CUSTARD! BULL'S-EYE! NICE JOB!
TROLLO LOLLO! WIDE TO THE RIGHT! TIGHTEN UP YOUR THROW!
I HAVE TO SAY, PONYACCI LOOKS MUCH HAPPIER.
AND HE'S GOT STUDENTS COMING FROM ALL OVER EQUESTRIA! THE SCHOOL'S A HUGE SUCCESS!
GIGGLE FIT! WATCH YOUR AIM! YOU ALMOST HIT LAUGHING MATTER!
WHY DIDN'T YOU ASK TO JOIN, PINKIE?
I'M SURE PONYACCI WOULD LOVE TO TEACH YOU.
OH...
LET'S JUST SAY I'VE ALREADY LEARNED PLENTY FROM HIM.

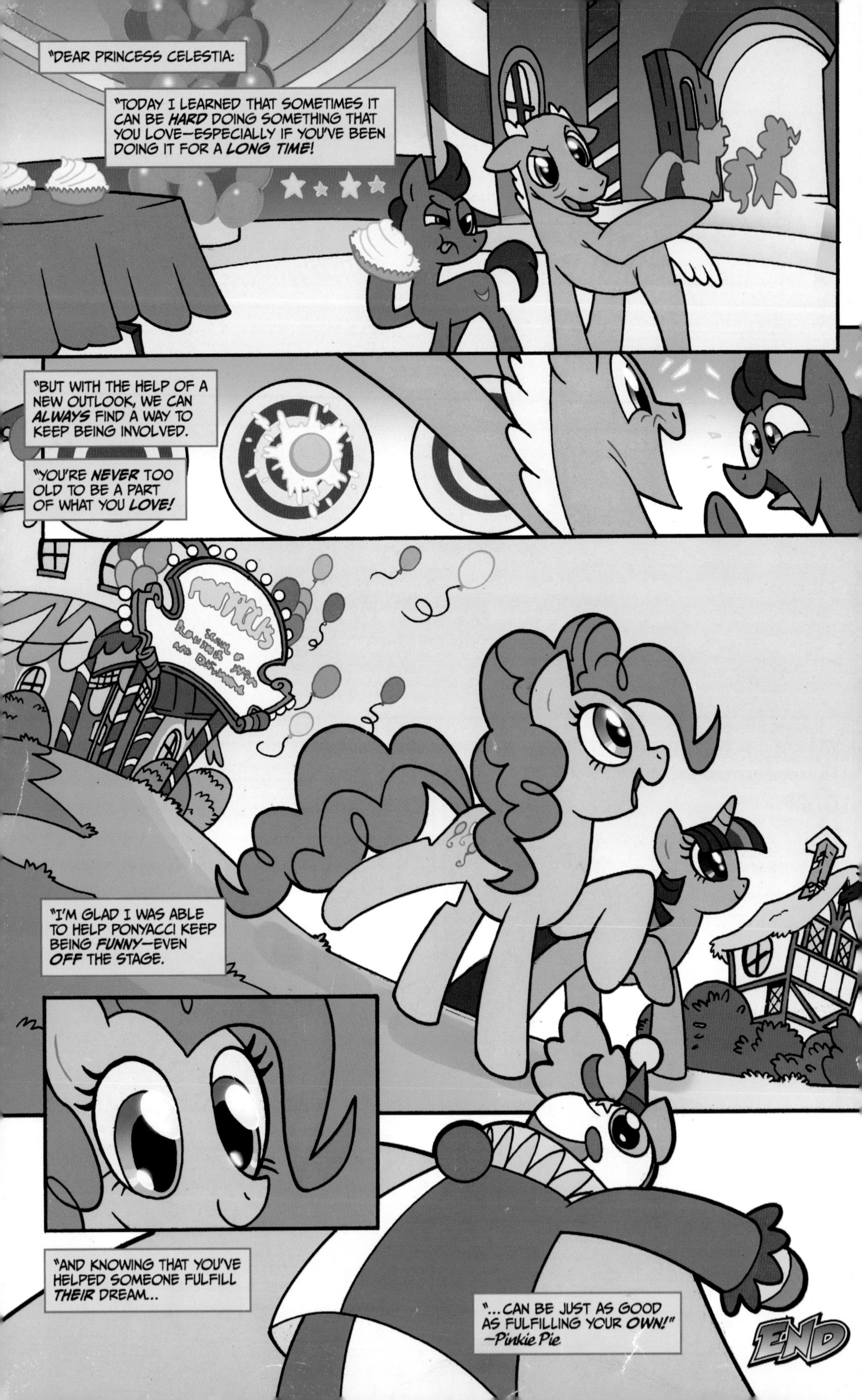

"DEAR PRINCESS CELESTIA:
"TODAY I LEARNED THAT SOMETIMES IT CAN BE HARD DOING SOMETHING THAT YOU LOVE—ESPECIALLY IF YOU'VE BEEN DOING IT FOR A LONG TIME!
"BUT WITH THE HELP OF A NEW OUTLOOK, WE CAN ALWAYS FIND A WAY TO KEEP BEING INVOLVED.
"YOU'RE NEVER TOO OLD TO BE A PART OF WHAT YOU LOVE!
"I'M GLAD I WAS ABLE TO HELP PONYACCI KEEP BEING FUNNY—EVEN OFF THE STAGE.
"AND KNOWING THAT YOU'VE HELPED SOMEONE FULFILL THEIR DREAM...
"...CAN BE JUST AS GOOD AS FULFILLING YOUR OWN!" —Pinkie Pie
END